HISTORY OF ROCK AND ROLL

THE REVOLUTION OF ROCK—
THE 1970s

Written by: Stuart A. Kallen
Edited by: Bob Italia

Published by Abdo & Daughters, 6537 Cecilia Circle, Bloomington, Minnesota 55435

Library bound edition distributed by Rockbottom Books, Pentagon Tower, P.O. Box 36036, Minneapolis, Minnesota 55435

Copyright© 1989 by Abdo Consulting Group, Inc., Pentagon Tower, P.O. Box 36036, Minneapolis, Minnesota 55435. International copyrights reserved in all countries. No part of this book may be reproduced in any form without written permission from the publisher. Printed in the United States.

Library of Congress Number: 89-084918   ISBN: 0-939179-76-8

Cover Photos by: Michael Ochs Archive
Inside Photos by: Michael Ochs Archive

THE SEVENTIES

As the 70s began, new technology was changing the face of music. Sounds and tones that the Beatles had labored for days to reproduce now could be achieved with the push of a button. The same type of recording equipment that the Beatles used on "Sgt. Pepper" was considered to be "prehistoric" only three years later. The studio became a place where the skills of a jet pilot were needed to operate the recording console.

All these technical advancements came with a price for Rock-n-Roll. The new equipment was expensive, and the people who operated it were highly paid. That meant the music had to turn a profit if the mega-recording companies were going to touch it. Gone were the days of endless experimenting in the studio. At $200 an hour for recording time, a band was expected to get in and out of the studio as fast as possible, and the records had to sell big. Music that was once called revolutionary now became "product" to be sold like cars or T.V.'s in the marketplace.

TAKE IT EASY

The musical reactions to the music industry were many and varied. The rise of acoustical oriented music like Crosby, Stills, Nash and Young, James Taylor, Joni Mitchell, Carol King and others, proved that all the electronic gadgetry in the world could not sound better than beautiful harmony, heartfelt singing and a good old guitar. This approach was taken one step further by bands like the Eagles, Poco and the Flying Burrito Bros. These groups merged pedal-steel guitar, violins and banjos with drums and guitar to forge a new sound called Country Rock.

CROSBY, STILLS, NASH & YOUNG

Formed out of some of the most popular folk-rock groups of the 60s, Crosby, Stills, Nash & Young seemed to be the wave of the future as the 70s dawned. Their sensitive lyrics, sung in tight four part harmony, seemed just the balm to heal America's youth, wounded by the raging war in Viet Nam.

Crosby, Stills, Nash & Young.

The group consisted of David Crosby, who started out in the Byrds, Stephen Stills from Buffalo Springfield and Graham Nash from the English group The Hollies. All these bands had number one hits in the 60s. Neil Young played in Buffalo Springfield, did solo albums, and joined CS&N on their second album.

In 1968, David Crosby and Stephen Stills were coasting on the millions they'd earned in the Byrds and Buffalo Springfield. Crosby had discovered Joni Mitchell in Florida, and soon she too was jamming with Crosby's friends like John Sebastion (from the Lovin' Spoonful) and Mama Cass Elliot (from the Mamas and Papas).

THE GREATEST HIGH HARMONY SINGER

Crosby and Stills felt that they were ready to make some records but they needed a high harmony to fill out their sound. John Sebastion said that the greatest high harmony singer he knew was Graham Nash. In England, Graham Nash was desperately trying to hold together The Hollies, a band he'd been in since his youth that had many chart topping hits in the 60s. After a particularly bad argument with the group one night, Graham decided to fly to L.A. and check out Stills and Crosby.

It didn't take Nash long to realize he'd made the right decision. When Crosby, Stills and Nash opened their mouths to sing, everyone within earshot was mesmerized. Soon the trio was in the studio recording their first album.

CSN & Y created a sound known to many as "Western Sky Music."

When the album, simply entitled "Crosby, Stills & Nash" came out in the summer of 1969, public reaction was immediate. Fueled by the single "Marrakesh Express," "Crosby, Stills & Nash" quickly rose up the charts. Jimi Hendrix called their sound "Western Sky Music."

FOUR WAY STREET

One afternoon, Neil Young was sitting in his incredible house, built up on stilts, in a woody canyon outside of L.A. When the doorbell rang, Neil opened the front door, and there was his ex-bandmate from Buffalo Springfield, Steve Stills. Stills asked Young to play with Crosby, Stills & Nash, but not as a band member, just as sort of a walk-on guest. Neil said, "Nothing doin' man, I want my name on it."
And that's how Neil Young got his name added to the most elite new band moniker on the scene: Crosby, Stills, Nash and Young! With the help of his old friends, Neil Young would go on to become the biggest star of them all.

WOODSTOCK NATION

The rain was pouring down, and the helicopter carrying CSN&Y bucked and pitched in the wind, just barely making a safe landing behind the fence seperating the stage from the 400,000 people. 400,000 people! If they weren't scared to death by the helicopter ride, they were sure scared now. This was their second concert!

At 3:00 o'clock in the morning, Crosby, Stills, Nash & Young finally took the stage. After the first emotionally charged chords of "Suite: Judy Blue Eyes", any fears the group had were washed away by the shouts and applause of the crowd.

DEJA VU

When the movie "Woodstock" came out, CSN&Y became megastars. With the release of their second album (their first with Neil), CSN&Y became one of the highest paid rock acts of the 70s. Throughout the 70s and 80s, there have been albums and tours with different pairings of CSN&Y. With another reunion in the works, it looks like David Crosby, Stephen Stills, Graham Nash and Neil Young will be pleasing audiences with great music for a "long time coming."

SOUTHERN ROCK

Rock-n-Roll was born in the southern part of the United States. All the early rockers from Muddy Waters to Elvis to Little Richard were from the South. During the 60s, rock music spread its wings everywhere, and the groups dominating the charts were from places like England, Detroit and San Francisco.

By the early 70s a new breed of musician had emerged from the South. By taking the roots of Blues and pumping it up with raw talent, the Allman Brothers planted the seeds of Southern boogie. Soon, an army of hard-charging bands like Lynyrd Skynyrd came out of the south. With their fiercely proud, down-home lyrics, backed up by virtuoso musicianship, these bands from Florida, Georgia and Alabama proved indeed that the South had risen again.

THE ROOTS OF HEAVY METAL

By the late 60s, the time was ripe for a bold, new musical sound. Advancements in electronics freed the guitarist from a small amplifier with a tinny speaker. By 1969, players like Peter Townshend of The Who were able to plug into a 3000 watt inferno of screaming feedback. Wah-wah pedals, distortion boxes and phase shifters became part of the guitar player's arsenal that shattered concert attendance records, if not a few eardrums.

The basic Blues form was a perfect place for the new Superstars to ply their trade. The repeating chords and solid rhythm gave the drummers, bassists and guitarists plenty of room to stretch. Ten minute guitar solos, followed by fifteen minute drum solos were the stock in trade of bands like Cream and Iron Butterfly. Since the 1950's the tinny pop started by Blues greats such as Muddy Waters and Willie Dixon has grown into a fiery explosion of sound known as Heavy Metal.

ERIC CLAPTON —
GUITAR LEGEND IN HIS OWN TIME

When Eric Clapton quit the Yardbirds in 1965, people thought he had made a big mistake. The Yardbirds had just scored their first big hit with

"For Your Love", and their future looked rosy. After all, what could be better than to be an English pop star in the middle of the Beatles inspired "British Invasion?" But pop stardom and hit records were not important to Clapton. What was important to him was the pure and personal sound of the Blues.

CLAPTON IS GOD

After the Yardbirds, Eric teamed up with John Mayall's Bluesbreakers. Mayall was known for being a gifted band leader and many English superstars started their careers with a stint in Mayall's band. During his period as a Bluesbreaker, Clapton's playing style fell strictly within the bounds of pure blues. Audiences took notice of Eric, and soon London's subway stations were painted with graffiti saying "Clapton is God!" Quite an ego boost for a twenty-one year old guitar player.

But Clapton was restless. In another move that would cause many people to wonder about his sanity, Clapton quit the Bluesbreakers in 1966. Eric wanted to become a star in America, where the Blues were born.

Eric Clapton, a master of rock guitar.

THE CREAM OF THE CROP

Out of the thriving music scene in London, three men came together and hammered out a new musical sound on the anvil of the Blues. Eric Clapton joined with bassist Jack Bruce and drummer Ginger Baker. Unfortunately, the three of them had tempers and egos big enough to bring down the sky, and when they played together it seemed to a few people that the sky *was* falling!

The new band was christened "Cream," and after the release of "Sunshine of Your Love," Cream became rock's first "supergroup." On stage, Cream would take a basic blues song like "Crossroads," and turn it into a hurricane of thundering sound. Baker's merciless pounding, Bruce's throbbing bass runs and Clapton's gravity defying guitar licks sounded like three people soloing at once. All the previous boundaries of Rock-n-Roll were sacrificed under the axes of Cream. The albums "Disraeli Gears" and "Wheels of Fire" show Cream at their best.

Like a shooting star, Cream left a beautiful trail of music across the sky, and then fizzled out from its own brilliance. Barely three years old, but torn apart by personality clashes, Cream called it quits in 1968.

Out of the ashes of Cream, Clapton had a new vision. No superstars, no hype, just great music. Getting together with his old friend, keyboardist Steve Winwood, and bassist Rick Gretch, Clapton started Blind Faith. Windwood had been in the Spencer Davis Group when their version of "I'm a Man" made him a seventeen year old star. After playing with Traffic for three years, Windwood was glad to find a new direction with Clapton. Today Windwood is one of the biggest solo artists in the music industry.

When ex-Cream drummer, Ginger Baker, was added to the line-up, Blind Faith went the route of Clapton's other bands-they had a very successful album and then broke up.

LAYLA

For about a year, Clapton, tired of being on the center stage, became a sideman for Delaney and Bonnie, a British R & B outfit. After playing a concert with John Lennon's Plastic Ono Band in 1970, Clapton formed Derek and the Dominos. The Dominos scored what was perhaps Clapton's biggest hit with "Layla," a song about George Harrison's wife whom Eric had become romantically involved.

Clapton's wealth and fame could not buy him happiness, and as the 70s progressed, Eric slid deeper and deeper into the destructive world of hard drugs.

Although he never regained the thunder he had with his previous bands, Clapton, having licked his bad habits, still records and tours in the 90s. The recently released "Crossroads" is a five album compilation of twenty years worth of Clapton genius. "Crossroads" proves to any doubtful listener that Eric Clapton is one of the founding fathers of Heavy Metal Rock.

JIMI HENDRIX — PIONEER OF HEAVY METAL

The crowd at the Monterey Pop Festival was going insane! The dude up on stage allowed no other reaction. Wearing a wide headband, practically dripping with buckles, beads and feather boas, Jimi Hendrix was playing the guitar with his teeth! The wall of Marshall amplifiers

Jimi Hendrix was a pioneer of heavy metal.

behind him screeched and groaned, shaking with the vibration of a hundred notes all played at once. Some in the crowd wondered just what planet this guy was from! At the end of "Wild Thing," Hendrix whips off his Stratocaster, drops to his knees, and straddling the thing, pulls out a can of Zippo lighter fluid. After hosing down his guitar with the fluid, Hendrix starts it on fire! The Strat screams for mercy as it burns. Welcome to the Jimi Hendrix Experience's first American concert.

An ancient Chinese proverb says, "A journey of a thousand miles begins with the first step." If the flashing, thundering, sonic-boom, known as "Metal" in the 90s, is a thousand mile journey, then Jimi Hendrix was the first step.

HE PLAYED IT BOTH WAYS

James Marshall Hendrix was born on November 27, 1942, in Seattle, Washington. His mother Lucille died when he was ten. His father, James Allen Hendrix, worked as a landscape gardener and had a large collection of Blues and R & B records. When Jimi was 12, his dad bought him a guitar to replace the broom he'd been strumming.

Jimi would watch other guitar players and imitate what they were doing. Hendrix was ambidextrous, which means he could write or play guitar right-handed or left-handed. Jimi favored his left hand, and usually played his right-handed Stratocaster upside down. Jimi also had perfect pitch, so when he heard music playing, he knew what notes were being played, just by listening.

When Jimi was 17, he was tired of the Seattle music scene. Jimi decided to see the world, so he joined the 101st Airborn Division of the U.S. Army. After 26 months in the service, Jimi hurt his back and his foot jumping out of an airplane. Soon Hendrix was once again a guitar-slinging civilian.

HAVE YOU EVER BEEN EXPERIENCED?

In the early 60s, Hendrix had earned a name for himself playing guitar with R & B greats like B.B. King, Ike and Tina Turner, Wilson Pickett and King Curtis. In 1965, Hendrix changed his name to Jimmy James and started his own group, The Blue Flames. Jimmy James and the Blue Flames played in New York City, and Jimi was gaining

When Jimi played, people listened.

notice with big time artists like Dylan and the Beatles.

One of the people who noticed this flamboyant, young guitar player was Chas Chandler. Chandler was the former bass player in the English group The Animals who had hits with "House of the Rising Sun" and "We Gotta Get Out Of This Place." Chandler was so impressed by Hendrix that he sold his bass guitar so he could buy Jimi some new equipment. Soon Chas handed Jimi some money, a plane ticket to England, and a promise to meet Eric Clapton. Jimi called his dad and said, "They're going to make me a star."

In England, Chandler paired Jimi with Mitch Mitchell, a drummer, and Noel Redding, a lead guitarist turned bass player. The new group was called The Jimi Hendrix Experience. The Experience became a huge hit in Europe after the release of "Purple Haze" in early 1967. America hadn't yet fallen under the spell of the "Voodoo Child."

BOLD AS LOVE

After Jimi's pyrotechnics at the Monterey Pop Festival (described at the beginning of this chapter), he was an instant star in America. Jimi recorded the albums "Have You Ever Been Experienced?", "Axis-Bold As Love" and "Electric Ladyland" within the next two years. Hendrix played to sold out crowds all over the world in 1968 and 1969.

By Jimi's 26th birthday, The Jimi Hendrix Experience was finished. Their excruciating touring schedule had taken its toll on the band members. Hendrix formed a new band with Buddy Miles and Billy Cox. They recorded their only album, "Band Of Gypsys" live at the Fillmore East in New York City.

AND THE SKY CAME TUMBLING DOWN

Jimi became more and more depressed by the music business. At a Band Of Gypsys concert in Madison Square Garden, Jimi walked off stage during the second song, leaving behind 19,000 disappointed fans.

By 1970, there was talk of reforming the Jimi Hendrix Experience and going on tour. All these plans came crashing to a permanent halt on September 17, 1970, when Jimi Hendrix was pronounced dead at St. Mary Abbot's Hospital in London. Jimi had accidentally overdosed on sleeping pills. There was some question as to the medical attention Hendrix received. Jimi was placed in the sitting position with his head back. The pills weren't enough to kill him, but with his head thrown back he couldn't breath, and he choked to death. By all accounts Jimi's death was a tragic and avoidable mistake.

After Jimi's death, scores of albums were released by his record company. Some show Hendrix's brilliance, some are studio throw aways that Jimi never would have released if he were alive. Jimi Hendrix also appeared in the movies "Monterey Pop", "Woodstock" and "Rainbow Bridge." Most video stores have these movies available for rental or sale.

The world mourned the passing of Rock's shining light. Before his 28th birthday, Jimi Hendrix had reshaped Rock-n-Roll beyond recognition. When he lit his guitar on fire at Monterey Pop, Jimi also lit a fire under millions of guitar players. From Led Zeppelin to Van Halen to Metallica, there isn't one Heavy Metal guitarist who didn't learn from the master of them all, Jimi Hendrix.

LED ZEPPELIN — MASTERS OF HEAVY METAL

When Jimmy Page told The Who's drummer, Keith Moon, that he was going to start a band, Keith replied, "That should go over like a lead zeppelin." Lead is the heaviest metal, and Led Zeppelin is one of the heaviest of the Heavy Metal bands. Composed of Jimmy Page, lead guitar, Robert Plant, vocals, John Bonham, drums, and John Paul Jones, bass and keyboards, Led Zeppelin has sold tens of millions of records worldwide.

Led Zeppelin was the brainchild of Jimmy Page. Page was a very well-known session musician in England in the mid-sixties. His playing can be heard on the records of The Kinks, The Who, Herman's Hermits, and countless others. Jimmy got tired of working behind the scenes and joined The Yardbirds in 1966 as a bass player. When the Yardbirds lead guitarist, Jeff Beck, quit the band, Page became the group's lead player. The Yardbirds had their difficulties, and soon Page was left with the band's famous name, but no musicians to play in it. Determined to save The Yardbirds, Page set out on a quest for fresh musicians for The New Yardbirds.

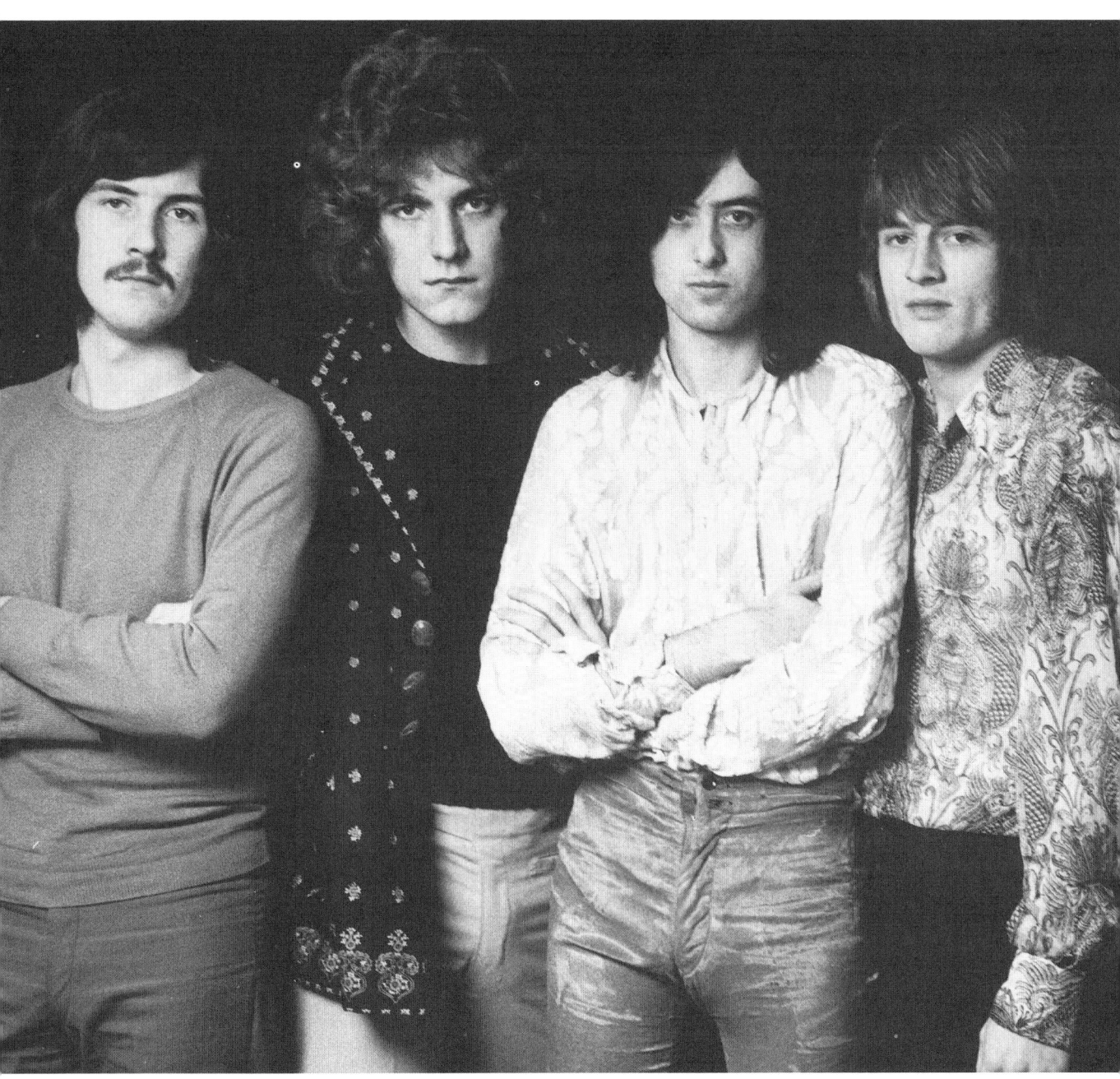

Led Zeppelin took heavy metal to new heights.

When Jimmy heard Robert Plant singing with his unknown group, Obbstweedle, he knew he had found one quarter of The New Yardbirds. Plant had an incredibly high, soulful voice, and the good looks needed to front a band. Plant recommended an old friend of his to fill the drummer's spot, John "Bonzo" Bonham. Page was amazed when he heard the wild thrashing of Bonzo's drumming, and signed him immediately. After recruiting another well-known sessions player, John Paul Jones on bass, The New Yardbirds were ready to fly. After a tour of Scandinavia, the group decided to drop The New Yardbirds name, and using Keith Moon's joke for a name, Led Zeppelin was born. Their first concert in London won them two standing ovations, several encores and rave reviews from the press.

STAIRWAY TO NUMBER ONE

When "Led Zeppelin I" was released in 1969, it rocketed straight to the top of the charts. That success was repeated six months later with "Led Zeppelin II." "Led Zeppelin III" and "IV" both went platinum, and Zeppelin astounded the world when they released the all time classic, "Stairway to Heaven." "Stairway to Heaven" has been in continual rotation on Rock radio stations for almost 20 years!

Led Zeppelin continued to tour and record throughout the 70s, selling millions of records and concert tickets. In 1976, Zeppelin released "The Song Remains the Same," a movie showing the explosive power of Led Zeppelin in concert. That movie is now available at most video outlets.

ZEPPELIN FLIES AWAY

In September of 1980, while on break from a recording session, John Bonham died of a heart attack brought on by excessive drinking. The band had just completed a sellout tour of Europe, and were working on a new album. After Bonham's death, a simple press release announced the end of Led Zeppelin.

Led Zeppelin left a legacy of style and talent. Heavy Metal bands come and go, some using the Zeppelin techniques successfully, some picking up where Zeppelin left off. But no matter what Metal band is at the top of the charts today, they all owe a debt to the magical pioneers of Heavy Metal: Led Zeppelin.

THE BRITISH INVASION (PART TWO)

In the late 60s, the Beatles inspired hundreds of English bands with their synthesis of rock and classical music. Called Art Rock or Classical Rock, bands like Procol Harum found that they could have number one hits by combining Bach Preludes with Rock poetry. "A Whiter Shade of Pale," by Procol Harum, gave other bands the cue. Classically trained musicians in Emerson, Lake and Palmer, Yes, Genesis, King Crimson and others, paved the way for yet another variation of good old Rock-n-Roll.

THE MOODY BLUES — IN SEARCH OF THE LOST CHORD

The Moody Blues, formed in 1965, rode the first wave of the British invasion with the hit single, "Go Now." The group reformed in 1967, replacing guitarist Denny Laine (who later joined with Paul McCartney in Wings) with Justin Hayward and John Lodge. The band took an entirely different direction, and recorded their next album, "Days of Future Past," with the London Festival Orchestra. That album contained the song

"Nights in White Satin" which sold over a million copies when it was released as a single in 1972.

The Moody's became the masters of Classical Rock in the late 60s and early 70s. Using a new invention called the Mellotron, the ancestor of the synthesizer, the Moody Blues used orchestral sound effects, flutes, guitars and drums to take the listener on a trip to outer space. Their songs, filled with spiritual imagery and beautiful flowing melodies, portrayed a world of fantastic gardens where people could become one with the universe. At the end of the 60s, people were ready to take such musical journeys, and the albums "In Search of the Lost Chord," "On the Threshold of a Dream," "To Our Children's Children" and "A Question of Balance" were eagerly snapped up by the Moody's fans.

After "Seventh Sojourn" in 1972, the Moody Blues took a six year break. When "Long Distance Voyager" came out in 1980, the Moody's returned to the number one slot. With the release of "Surlamer" in 1988, the Moody's have sold over 50 million records. And fortunately for their listeners, The Moody Blues are still searching for the lost chord.

JETHRO TULL — ENGLISH FOLK-ROCK

Jethro Tull, along with Fairport Convention and Steeleye Span, is one of the handful of traditional English Folk-Rock bands. Formed in 1968 by flutist Ian Anderson, Jethro Tull's music is loosely based on English folk songs. Jethro Tull's music is a study in contrasts. A song may start out with an acoustic guitar and flute playing a melody from the 14th Century. Suddenly the rest of the band kicks in with fuzz toned guitar, keyboards and a jazzy rhythm section. In the middle of it all is Ian Anderson, hopping around on one foot, dressed like a mad court jester, blowing crazily into his silver flute.

Jethro Tull is mainly thought of as a 70s band, but two of their best albums, "Stand Up" and "Benefit," were released in the late 60s. When "Aqualung" was released in 1971, Jethro Tull became Superstars. Several of Tull's albums have not sold well, and changing personel have caused the band some setbacks, but Ian Anderson has many a trick up his sleeve. There is little doubt that the world will once again hear from the "minstrel in the gallery" with his exciting brand of Rock-n-Roll.

PINK FLOYD — MUSIC FROM THE DARK SIDE OF THE MOON

"Which one's Pink?", a British music executive once asked Dave Gilmore, Pink Floyd's stellar guitarist. Once again, Gilmore explained that Pink Floyd's name came from combining the names of two Georgia Blues musicians. Pink Floyd's founder, Syd Barrett, loved the blues music of Pink Anderson and Floyd Council. When Barrett's band started playing their unique brand of cosmic space-rock, Syd playfully merged together the Bluesman's names and Pink Floyd was born.

During his early college years, Roger Waters, Pink Floyd's bassist, formed a band with Nick Mason on drums, and Richard Wright on keyboards. The band called itself various names including Meggadeath and The Screeming Abdabs. When Waters' old high school friend, Syd Barrett, joined the band, Barrett coined the name The Pink Floyd Sound. By the time the group was stunning the audiences in London's hippie underground scene, they were known simply as Pink Floyd.

Pink Floyd's early use of musical experimentation and sound effects guaranteed them notice by the record companies, and in 1967, they were signed by the Beatles recording company, EMI. Floyd's first album, "Piper At The Gates Of Dawn" features Barrett's fairy tale songs, sometimes innocent, sometimes threatening. With the use of electronic gadgets, Pink Floyd took simple songs and put them into the stratosphere. In concert, Pink Floyd used quadrophonic sound, smoke bombs and light shows to mesmerize their audience.

THE LUNATIC IS ON THE GRASS

By the winter of 1967, Syd Barrett's personality had taken a turn for the worse. Syd became very unpredictable at concerts. Sometimes he would stand motionless for hours while the band played, sometimes he would babble incoherently. When Barrett had a nervous breakdown in February 1968, he was replaced by a talented guitarist named Dave Gilmore.

With Gilmore on guitar, Pink Floyd "set the controls for the heart of the sun." Touring the U.S. and Europe, Pink Floyd developed a cult

Pink Floyds live concerts were a spectacle of light and sound.

following, devoted to the band's brand of psychedelic rock. Pink Floyd continued with their experimental music on the albums "Ummagumma," "Atom Heart Mother" and "Meddle." When new sound technology was invented, Pink Floyd worked it into their stage shows, dazzling their small but loyal audience. To broaden their horizons, Floyd also did movie soundtracks for the films "More," "The Valley" and "Zabriski Point."

ALL IN ALL —
ANOTHER BRICK IN THE WALL

All the years of recording and touring finally paid off for Pink Floyd with the release of "The Dark Side Of The Moon." Backing up Roger Waters' dark songs about life and death with amazingly high quality production, Pink Floyd became the biggest of the big. Dave Gilmore's "Money" put Floyd on the American singles charts for the first time. Fifteen years after its release, in May 1988, "The Dark Side Of The Moon" had been on Billboards Album Charts for an astounding **726 weeks!**

By the time of the "Animals" world tour in 1978, Roger Waters was becoming very unhappy about life as a Rock Star. After many months of hard work and little sleep, Waters was in severe emotional pain. Under this stress, Waters wrote most of the brutally revealing music for "The Wall."

Waters and Gilmore sent the basic track of "Another Brick in the Wall" to an engineer in North London, where the singing of children 10 to 15 year's old filled up the 24 tracks. When "Another Brick in the Wall" was released, it gave Pink Floyd their first number one single in the U.S. In 1982, a movie of "The Wall" was released, starring Bob Geldof as "Pink."

FINAL CUT

As Roger Waters' songwriting got bleeker and bleeker, his ego got bigger and bigger. After Waters fired drummer Nick Mason and keyboardist Richard Wright, Pink Floyd disbanded. Waters released a solo album in 1984. In 1987, Wright, Mason and Gilmore fired up Pink Floyd once again and released "A Momentary Lapse of Reason." A sellout world tour came on the heels of the album, putting Pink Floyd in the limelight once again. Roger Waters sued Floyd over the use of the name and that lawsuit will probably be tied up in court for years.

Whoever owns the name, Pink Floyd has spent over twenty years breaking the bounds of experimental music. They have gone from the London underground to unparalled world stardom. Pink Floyd has set the standard for quality in recording and live concerts. One hopes that the group will continue to record well into the 21st century, because there will never be another Pink Floyd.

ELTON JOHN — ROCK'S CAPTAIN FANTASTIC

The floodlights sweep the stage as 25,000 cheering fans rise to their feet. The spotlight hits a man descending a stairway in the center of the stage. Wearing six-inch, platform heeled shoes and dressed from head to toe in sequins and ostrich feathers, he teeters over to the white piano. In case someone didn't know who he was, the flashing oversized glasses perched on his nose spell his name, "Elton."

Eltons' performances are second to none.

Elton John was born Reginald Kenneth Dwight, in Middlesex, England on March 25, 1947. Elton was an only child, and his strict father discouraged him from playing music or sports. By the time the chubby, 10 year old's parents divorced, Elton had six years of piano playing under his belt. Without his father around, Elton was allowed to listen to Elvis Presley and other early Rockers.

By 1967, Elton was playing gigs all over Europe, backing up a blues singer named Long John Baldry. Tired of the grind, Elton auditioned for a company looking for "songwriters and talent." After being rejected, Elton was leaving the audition when a producer thrust a handful of papers at him. "Here," he said, "take these. They're lyrics by a man named Bernie Taupin." And so, one of the greatest songwriting teams of the 70s was born. (Elton and Bernie did all of their early songwriting by mail.)

When the album "Elton John" rose to number 45 in England, John decided to tour the U.S. to drum up support for his debut effort. Elton created quite a stir when he arrived at The Troubador, an

L.A. folk club, in a double-decker bus with "Elton John has arrived" written across the side. John was a natural showman, and soon "Your Song" reached number 8 on the U.S. charts.

Between 1971 and 1976 Elton became one of the most famous and highly paid solo performers in the Rock world. His stage shows and costumes grew more and more outrageous, earning himself the nickname, "The Liberace of Rock."

In 1974, Elton asked John Lennon if he could record "Lucy in the Sky With Diamonds." Lennon gave him permission to record the Beatles song and said if it reached number one, he would perform it with Elton in concert. When "Lucy" did reach number one, Lennon, true to his word, appeared with Elton at Madison Square Garden. That was John Lennon's last public performance.

Elton John took all the flash, feathers and sequins of 70s "Glamour Rock" and made them his own. Beneath his outrageous costumes beat the heart of a talented, sensitive musician. With his new music planned for 1989, Elton John is still one of Rock's guiding forces.

DAVID BOWIE — THE CHAMELEON OF ROCK-N-ROLL

The house lights dimmed in the crowded auditorium. From the dark stage, a grotesque, synthesized version of Beethoven's "Ode To Joy" throbbed through the sound system. Suddenly, dozens of strobe lights start flashing. The stuttering flashes keeping time to the weird music. The hush of the crowd turned into a roar as David Bowie and the Spiders From Mars rush out from backstage. The spotlights come up as Bowie pounds out the first chords to "Ziggy Stardust." Bowie is dressed like some bizarre creature from outer space from the souls of his red knee-high platform boots to the top of his carrot color hair. The Starman has arrived.

David Bowie was born David Jones on Elvis Presley's 12th birthday in London, England, on January 8, 1947. David learned saxophone in high school and played in several musical groups in his teen years. David changed his last name to Bowie so he would not be confused with Davy Jones of The Monkees. After flirting with Buddism and mime, Bowie released several albums in England with moderate success.

David Bowie, inventor of "Glam Rock."

ZIGGY PLAYED GUITAR

When "Ziggy Stardust" was released in 1972, Bowie took the world by storm. Bowie became Ziggy, the Rock Megastar destroyed by his own popularity. Using outrageous costumes and elaborate stage production, Bowie single-handedly created a new musical trend called "Glamour Rock" or "Glam Rock." Dozens of bands like the "New York Dolls" and "Mott the Hoople" followed Bowie's lead.

After the triumph of "Ziggy Stardust," Bowie broadened his horizons. He starred in the movie "The Man Who Fell To Earth" and acted in the stage play "The Elephant Man." Both rolls won rave reviews for Bowie as the world realized what a major talent he was. Bowie kept surprising his fans with each new album. "Diamond Dogs" was a gloomy album about the end of the world, "Young Americans" was a R & B/soul album (with John Lennon helping write and record the hit "Fame"). Bowie delved into the world of experimental music on his next several albums, "Low," "Station to Station" and "Heroes." In 1983, Bowie released "Let's Dance," his most commercial album in years. Through it all, Bowie starred in several movies and plays.

Like a chameleon changes its colors to blend in with its background, David Bowie has spent the years changing his image to fit in with Rock-n-Roll's many shapes and colors. Whether Bowie took on the image of Ziggy Stardust, The Thin White Duke, or the Elephant Man, Bowie's extraordinary talent as a musician and an actor have allowed him to reach for the stars again and again.

PUNK MUSIC — THE REVOLUTION IN ROCK

By the mid-seventies, popular music had become a slick, over-produced and boring form of music. A lot of people felt that the Superstars of the 70s had nothing to say to them personally. Left in the dust of the super-rich Glamour bands, the hopeless and unemployed teenagers in London were desperate for a sound of their own. Notorious hard-core bands like The Buzzcocks, The Clash and The Sex Pistols perfectly expressed the anger and frustration of these neglected kids.

Rock -n- Rolls angry revolutionist, The Sex Pistols.

THE SEX PISTOLS — PUNK'S ANGRY PIONEERS

The Sex Pistols were a creation of Macolm McLaren, a clothing store owner in London. After mis-managing The New York Dolls into bankruptcy, McLaren decided to take some kids hanging around his boutique and start a revolution.

In 1975, McLaren recruited Johnny Lydon, an unemployed janitor, who had never thought of playing music. McLaren changed Lydon's name to Johnny Rotten, and threw him in with guitarist Steve Jones, bassists Glen Matlock and drummer Paul Cook. Dubbing the band "The Sex Pistols," McLaren set about getting the band some gigs.

From the very beginning, The Sex Pistols attracted attention. They were ugly, they spit on their audience and they couldn't play music to save their lives! Their 1976 gigs showed a band full of violent energy who were anti-rockstar, anti-government and anti-everything else. In November of 1976, The Sex Pistols were signed by EMI. Their single "Anarchy in the U.K." earned them a spot on British television. After their obscene dialogue on T.V., The Sex Pistols

Johnny Rotten, punk rocks cult leader.

were front page news, and the Punk Revolution was born.

Rotten replaced Matlock with non-bassist Sid Vicious, but by then, the Pistols were banned from everywhere. Several more recordings earned The Sex Pistols a place in history. After an American tour where the band was severely beaten-up in Texas, Rotten announced the breakup of The Sex Pistols. The other three tried to keep the Pistols alive, but the band was doomed. After several disasterous gigs, Sid Vicious was arrested for stabbing his girlfriend to death. Sid died of an overdose while awaiting trial.

The Sex Pistols lacked musical talent, but they woke up the slumbering giant of the music industry. Established Superstars were forced to breath some fresh air into their stale music. The Punk revolution also spawned New Wave Music. Bands like The Police, The Talking Heads and The Cars all use a back-to-the-basics approach to Rock-n-Roll. In the end, The Sex Pistols proved that Rock-n-Roll belongs to everybody, and as Sid Vicious sang, "I did it my way."

BIBLIOGRAPHY

Bronson, Fred. **The Billboard Book of Number One Hits.** New York: Billboard Publications, 1988.

Carr, Roy and Murray, Charles Shaar. **David Bowie.** New York: Avon Books, 1981.

Clifford, Mike. **The Harmony Illustrated Encyclopedia of Rock.** New York: Harmony Books, 1985.

Coleman, Ray. **Clapton!** New York: Warner Books, 1985.

Davis, Stephen. **Hammer of the Gods.** New York: William Morrow and Company Inc., 1985.

Edwards, Henry and Zanetta, Tony. **Stardust.** New York: McGraw-Hill Book Co., 1986.

Fornatale, Pete. **The Story of Rock 'n' Roll.** New York: William Morrow and Co., Inc., 1987.

Obrecht, Has. **Masters of Heavy Metal.** New York: Quill/A Guitar Player Book, 1984.

Santelli, Robert. **Sixties Rock.** Chicago: Contemporary Books, Inc., 1985.

Superstars of the 70's. London: Octopus Books, 1975.

Ward, Ed and Stokes, Geoffrey and Tucker, Ken. **Rock of Ages.** New York: Rolling Stone Press/Summit Books, 1986.

Zimmer, Dave and Diltz, Henry. **Crosby, Stills & Nash.** New York: St. Martin's Press, 1985.